Farmer Joe Baby-Sits

by **Nancy Wilcox Richards**

illustrated by
Werner Zimmermann

Scholastic Canada Ltd.
Toronto New York London Auckland Sydney
Mexico City New Delhi Hong Kong Buenos Aires

With love, to Jenn and Kris
with special blanket memories.
– N. W. R.

To the mysterious woman on the plane from Antigua, Linda
Knowles, and the crazy, zany and always helpful Stocktons.
– W. Z.

Scholastic Canada Ltd.
604 King Street West, Toronto, Ontario M5V 1E1, Canada

Scholastic Inc.
557 Broadway, New York, NY 10012, USA

Scholastic Australia Pty Limited
PO Box 579, Gosford, NSW 2250, Australia

Scholastic New Zealand Limited
Private Bag 94407, Botany, Manukau 2163, New Zealand

Scholastic Children's Books
Euston House, 24 Eversholt Street, London NW1 1DB, UK

The illustrations were painted in watercolours on Arches paper.

Library and Archives Canada Cataloguing in Publication
Richards, Nancy Wilcox, 1958-
Farmer Joe baby-sits / by Nancy Wilcox Richards ; illustrations by Werner Zimmermann.
ISBN 978-1-4431-1377-9
I. Zimmermann, H. Werner (Heinz Werner), 1951- II. Title.
PS8585.I184F16 2012   jC813'.54   C2011-908101-6

6 5 4 3 2 1   Printed in Singapore 46   12 13 14 15 16

Farmer Joe lived with his wife
in an old house
in the middle of a big field.

1

Most days Farmer Joe
worked hard in the field.
He cut the wheat.
He planted the corn.
He pulled the weeds.

But not today.
Today was a special day.
Farmer Joe was going to baby-sit Jennifer.

Farmer Joe had never done any baby-sitting
before in his whole life!

Jennifer's mother brought a huge bag of toys
and a long list of instructions for Farmer Joe:

  Play lots of games.
  Give Jennifer a snack.
  Make sure she gets outside
  for some fresh air.

And on the very bottom of the list:

  Make sure Jennifer has an afternoon nap.
  She will need her blanket,
  otherwise she WON'T sleep.

Bumpity-bump-bump-bump
went the truck down the dirt road.

Farmer Joe and Jennifer were alone.

Farmer Joe was puzzled about all the toys,
so he decided to show Jennifer his farm, instead.
They went outside and walked through
this field and that.

They crawled under and over fences.
They climbed up and down ladders.

When they got back to the old house
Farmer Joe decided it was time for
Jennifer's nap.

But where was her blanket?

He pulled out books, puzzles and dolls,
tutus, markers and balls . . .
but no blanket.

Jennifer found skates, a hoop and a tea set,
crayons and paints and a helmet . . .
but no blanket.

Oh, no!

"I know," Farmer Joe exclaimed.
"We must have lost your blanket
somewhere outside.
It should be easy to find. Let's go!"

Farmer Joe and Jennifer
walked through the fields.
They found some corn that
needed planting,
and a cow that needed milking.

They found a wagon that needed painting . . .
but no blanket.

They found a ladder for climbing,
and a rope for swinging.

They found some eggs that needed collecting . . . but no blanket.

Farmer Joe was worried they would never find it. Jennifer was *sure* they wouldn't.

But Farmer Joe would not give up.
They walked through this field and that.
They crawled under and over fences.
They climbed up and down ladders.

They searched everywhere . . .
but no blanket.

"I am sorry, Jennifer," Farmer Joe sighed. "I know you can't nap without your blanket, but there is no place left to look."

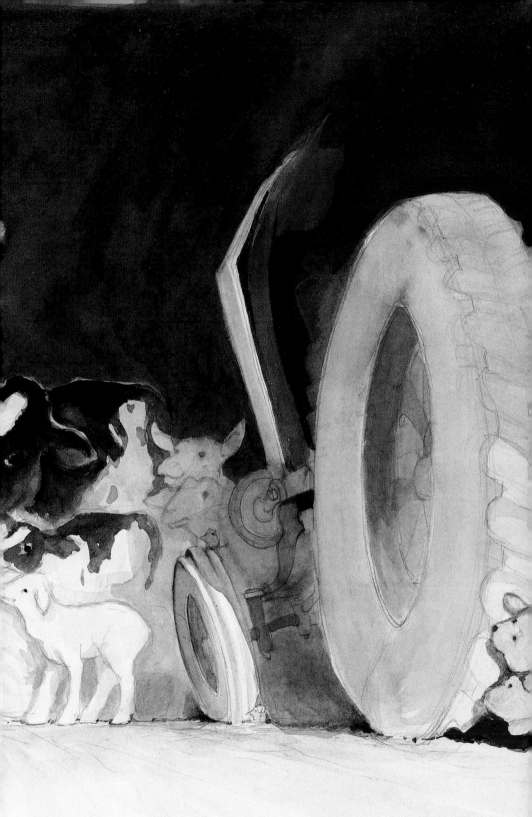

19

But Jennifer did not say anything.

Bumpity-bump-bump-bump
came the truck up the dirt road.

Farmer Joe felt a grin coming on.

"Sweet dreams, Jennifer," he whispered.

"Come back any time you like."